With love to Maya Wade,
M S.

Henry and the Huckleberries:
A Visit with Mr. Thoreau at Walden Pond

Based on a true story

Written by
Sally Sanford

Sally Sanford
March 5, 2017

Illustrated by Caldecott Honor winner
Ilse Plume

Ilse Plume

PROSPECTA PRESS
WESTPORT, CONNECTICUT ~ NEW YORK, NEW YORK

Our thanks to Jeffrey S. Cramer for pointing us to the story of the Huckleberry Party
and to the staff at the Thoreau Institute, especially Kathi Anderson and Matthew Burne,
for their assistance and for guiding us to the Pine Cobble path.
The journal entries of Henry David Thoreau in our story are taken
from *I to Myself: An Annotated Selection from the Journal of Henry D. Thoreau*, edited by Jeffrey S. Cramer.
~S.S.

Book design by Sally Sanford

Published by
Prospecta Press
P.O. Box 3131, Westport, CT 06880
203.571.0781   www.prospectapress.com

ISBN: 978-1-63226-076-5

FIRST EDITION, 2017

PRINTED IN CANADA

For my children, with love always
~ S.S.

To my daughter, Anne-Marie, and to the memory of my mother, Alice
~I.P.

"Cheerio, Cheerio" came a chirping from outside the cabin. Hearing the robin's morning greeting, Henry opened one eye to see the first light coming in the window. Henry smiled as he remembered that his young friends were coming for a Huckleberry Party today. The rosy dawn promised perfect weather for berry picking and a picnic.

Henry, now fully awake, looked around his very tiny one-room cabin in the woods by Walden Pond. He had built his little house himself. It had two windows, a door, a bed, a desk, a small table, three wooden chairs, and a fireplace.

Henry got up, dressed quickly, and walked down the short path to the pond.

The morning light glistened on the water. Henry knelt down and washed his face and hands. He loved this time of day and might have stayed longer by the shore, but he wanted to write in his journal before his visitors arrived, so he went up the path to his garden and picked some vegetables for breakfast.

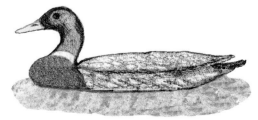

After breakfast, Henry started to write: 'August 6 — As I was walking along a hillside the other day, I smelled the minty scent of pennyroyal, but it was only after looking for quite sometime that I discovered I had stepped on it....' Just then he heard laughter, the clanging of berry pails, and voices outside—it was his young guests—so he went out to welcome them.

"Good morning to you, Mr. Thoreau!" they cried all at once.

"And a fine morning it is indeed, my friends. Hello Louisa—how is your father? And Monty, how is your garden growing? And who is this, why Edward, you look at least two inches taller since your last visit!"

As he was the youngest and smallest, Edward was especially pleased by Henry's observation.

The children showed Henry all the things they had collected during their short walk from town. Louisa had a tree branch that Henry quickly identified from its bundles of five needles as a white pine. Monty had leaves from a swamp maple already showing hints of red. And Edward pulled out of his pocket a tiny wood frog that quickly hopped out of his hand.

Eager to start their huckleberry hike, the children gathered their pails and the picnic basket that Edward's mother, Mrs. Emerson, had prepared for them, and they set off for Pine Cobble.

Along the way, Henry stopped to show them things he spotted: a turkey tail tree mushroom, white Indian pipes, and bright red partridge berries. He identified the birds they heard just from their songs: the white-throated sparrow singing "Oh sweet, Canada, Canada," the veery with its cascading trills, and the wood thrush with its flute-like flourishes.

Henry knew the woods around Walden better than anyone, and he knew all the good places to find huckleberries. The patch they soon came to was perfect for picking. The bushes were bursting with delicious, slightly tart, dark-blue berries. Inside each berry were ten edible seeds. The children quickly went to work filling their pails, occasionally popping a ripe berry into their mouths.

From the top of Pine Cobble, they had a magnificent view of Walden Pond and the mountains off in the distance.

They happily picked until their pails were full—Edward thinking about the delicious pie his mother would make, Louisa planning to give some berries to her neighbors and share the rest with her sisters, Monty imagining berries and cream for dessert, and Henry remembering when he was a boy and school closed for the day so that everyone could pick berries.

After picking so many berries, everyone was hungry. They found a nice spot under the shade of an oak tree where they enjoyed their simple picnic.

After lunch, Henry pulled a flute out of his pocket and began to play. Enchanted by the delicate music mingling with the songs of the birds and the gentle rustle of the trees, the children wished the magical moment could last forever.

It was time to head back. Henry put his flute away, and they tidied up, making sure they left no sign of disturbing the woods.

They picked up their pails and headed toward the path, Louisa running ahead with Monty close on her heels. Edward, trying to catch up to them, didn't see a large tree root and tripped, dropping his pail and scattering berries everywhere!

Edward's heart sank, his feelings hurting more than his skinned knee. He had spilled all the berries he had worked so hard to pick!

Edward began to cry. He couldn't stop crying. The more he tried, the harder he cried. Not sure what to say, Louisa quietly gave him her handkerchief.

Henry went over to Edward and spoke to him gently.

"Why, Edward, what a wonderful thing has happened! If huckleberry crops are going to continue, some of the berries have to be scattered from time to time. Nature has provided that little boys should now and then stumble and sow the berries, just as you have done. We shall have a grand lot of bushes in this spot, and we shall owe them to you."

Edward stopped crying and began to smile. Louisa gave him some of her berries. Thinking of all the berries sprouting up on Pine Cobble next summer, Edward smiled all the way back to the pond.

The late afternoon shadows stretching over the pond rippled in the breeze, while the children waded in the water to cool off.

Then they put
on their shoes
and thanked
"Mr. Thoreau"
for the best
Huckleberry Party
ever, promising to
return soon.
Henry waved as
they clambered
along the path
toward town.

Sunset that evening was one of Nature's most glorious.
Everything was quiet and still, except for the soft jingling of the
summer peepers. Henry loved this time of day. He felt joined
with the woods, the sky, and the water in a special way.

In the fading light, he walked slowly up to the cabin.

After supper, Henry lit a candle and took out his journal. He wrote: 'A boy spilled his huckleberries today. I saw that Nature was making use of him to disperse her berries, and I might have advised him to pick another pail full.'

At their homes, Henry's young friends tumbled into bed and went to sleep almost immediately, but not before Edward smiled once more at the thought of all the huckleberries that would grow in the spot where he had dropped his pail.

AUTHOR'S NOTE

This story is based on an actual "Huckleberry Party" that is recounted both in Henry David Thoreau's journal (from which I have quoted) and in Moncure Conway's autobiography. Using a "reality fiction" story-telling technique frequently employed by Louisa May Alcott, I have added "Louisa" to the story, as she was a frequent visitor to Henry David Thoreau's cabin at Walden and went berry picking with Mr. Thoreau on many occasions. Thoreau taught Louisa a great deal about the natural world and also about the rich world of the imagination. She would incorporate the two in her first published book, *Flower Fables*, and later wrote a chapter called "Huckleberries" in *Little Men*. Edward is based on Edward Emerson, the son of Ralph Waldo Emerson, who was nine at the time of his huckleberry mishap. I have given Moncure Conway the nickname "Monty." I have also quoted Mr. Thoreau from Conway's account of the Huckleberry Party included in Jeffrey S. Cramer's *I to Myself: An Annotated Selection from the Journal of Henry D. Thoreau*. For more background information and connections about the flora, fauna, and people in this story, please visit Henry and the Huckleberries on Facebook or visit www.henryandthehuckleberries.com.

Sally Sanford, *Concord, Massachusetts*